Stephanie Cabral

DEE SNIDER is best known as the lead singer and songwriter of the eighties sensation Twisted Sister, and has gone on to an eclectic career in radio, television, and film, as a writer and performer on Broadway, and as a social activist. He continues to write music and perform throughout the world.

Visit www.akashicbooks.com/author/dee-snider/ for a more detailed accounting of his remarkable and varied career.

MARGARET MCCARTNEY (illustrator) grew up in Washington, DC, where she played flute in the Police Boys & Girls Club Band and guitar in the band Tuscadero. She has met both Bill Clinton and Jimmy Walker. She studied illustration at the Rhode Island School of Design. Her work has appeared on everything from garden gloves to comics to her own line of children's wear, Winter Water Factory. She lives and works in Brooklyn, New York. She enjoys fiction and dumplings.

"We're Not Gonna Take It"
Written by Daniel "Dee" Snider
Courtesy of Universal Tunes
Used by Permission. All Rights Reserved.

LyricPop is a children's picture book collection by LyricVerse and Akashic Books.

lyricverse.

Published by Akashic Books
Song lyrics ©1984 Daniel "Dee" Snider
Illustrations ©2020 Margaret McCartney

ISBN: 978-1-61775-788-4
Library of Congress Control Number: 2019949646
First printing

Printed in Malaysia

Akashic Books
Brooklyn, New York, USA
Ballydehob, Co. Cork, Ireland
Twitter: @AkashicBooks
Facebook: AkashicBooks
E-mail: info@akashicbooks.com
Website: www.akashicbooks.com

SONG LYRICS BY

DEE SNIDER

ILLUSTRATIONS BY MARGARET McCARTNEY

We're not gonna take it

No, we ain't gonna take it

We're not gonna take it

anymore!

We've got the right to choose it

**There ain't no way we'll lose it
This is our life, this is our song**

**We'll fight the powers that be, just
Don't pick our destiny 'cause
You don't know us, you don't belong**

We're not gonna take it
No, we ain't gonna take it
We're not gonna take it anymore

**Oh, you're so condescending
Your gall is never-ending
We don't want nothin',**

not a thing from you

Your life is trite and jaded
Boring and confiscated

If that's your best, your best won't do

Whoa, oh oh
Whoa, oh oh

We're right (yeah)   **We'll fight (yeah)**
We're free (yeah)   **You'll see**

Whoa, whoa, we're not gonna take it
No, we ain't gonna take it
We're not gonna take it anymore

We're not gonna take it

**No,
we ain't
gonna take it**

We're not
gonna take it

anymore

No way!

We're right (yeah)
We're free (yeah)
We'll fight (yeah)

You'll see

No, we ain't gonna take it

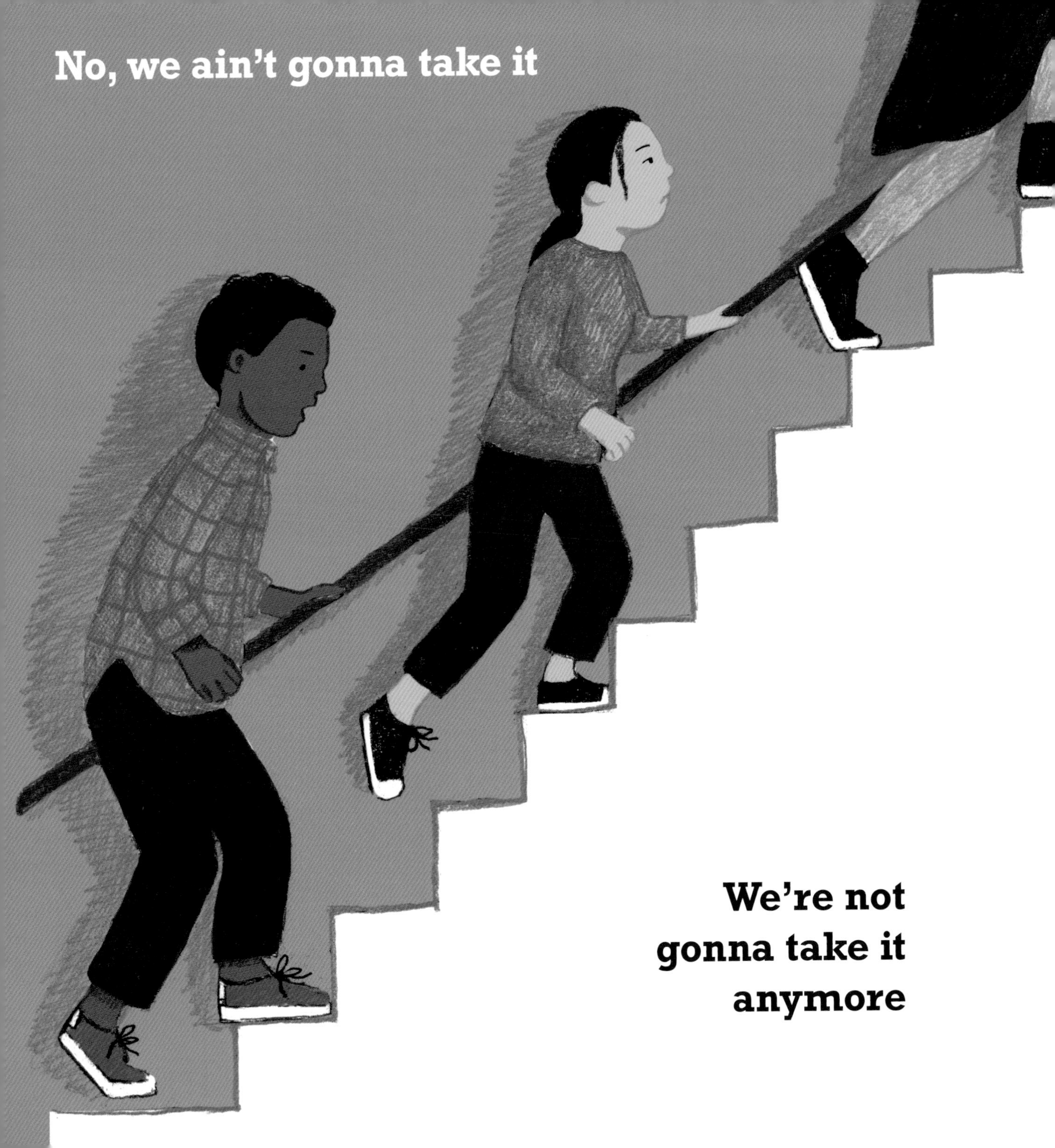

We're not
gonna take it
anymore

We’re not gonna take it

No, we ain’t gonna take it

We’re not gonna take it anymore

We're not gonna take it
No, we ain't gonna take it
We're not gonna take it anymore

Also available from **LyricPop**

GOOD VIBRATIONS
Song lyrics by Mike Love and Brian Wilson
Illustrations by Paul Hoppe
Mike Love and Brian Wilson's world-famous song, gloriously illustrated by Paul Hoppe, will bring smiles to the faces of children and parents alike.
Hardcover, $16.95, ISBN: 978-1-61775-787-7 | E-book, $16.99, 978-1-61775-833-1

DON'T STOP
Song lyrics by Christine McVie
Illustrations by Nusha Ashjaee
A beautifully illustrated picture book based on Christine McVie of Fleetwood Mac's enduring anthem to optimism and patience.
Hardcover, $16.95, ISBN: 978-1-61775-805-8 | E-book, $16.99, 978-1-61775-831-7

AFRICAN
Song lyrics by Peter Tosh
Illustrations by Rachel Moss
A beautiful children's picture book featuring the lyrics of Peter Tosh's global classic celebrating people of African descent.
Hardcover, $16.95, ISBN: 978-1-61775-799-0 | E-book, $16.99, 978-1-61775-830-0